W9-BRC-455

THE DWARKS
MEET THE TRASH MONSTER

Granny rocked back and forth in her chair.

"The Trash Monster," she began, "is a huge, hairy creature. It has glowing red eyes, sharp white teeth, and long yellow claws."

"Ulp!" gulped the Dwarklets.

"By day," continued Granny, "it sleeps in its lair beneath the trash, but by night, it rises up to stalk the dump in search of food. It eats *anything*—bicycle tires, alley cats, Big Macs, vacuum cleaners, *and . . .* DWARKLETS!"

Bantam Skylark Books of Related Interest
Ask your bookseller for the books you have missed

THE BLUE-NOSED WITCH
by Margaret Embry
THE CHOCOLATE TOUCH
by Patrick Skene Catling
DETECTIVE POUFY'S FIRST CASE
by Charlotte Pomerantz
DON'T BE MAD, IVY by Christine McDonnell
THE DWARKS by Michael Berenstain
THE DWARKS MEET SKUNK MOMMA
by Michael Berenstain
THE DWARKS MEET THE TRASH MONSTER
by Michael Berenstain
THE FALLEN SPACEMAN by Lee Harding
THE GOOD-GUY CAKE by Barbara Dillon
HUGH PINE by Janwillem van de Wetering
JENNY'S CAT by Miska Miles
JENNY'S MOONLIGHT ADVENTURE
by Esther Averill
MUSTARD by Charlotte Graeber
QUIMBLE WOOD by N. M. Bodecker
THE ROQUEFORT GANG by Sandy Clifford
THE SCHOOL FOR CATS by Esther Averill
THE WHITE STALLION by Elizabeth Shub

THE DWARKS MEET THE TRASH MONSTER ·

Book 3
by Michael Berenstain

A BANTAM SKYLARK BOOK®
TORONTO · NEW YORK · LONDON · SYDNEY · AUCKLAND

RL 3, 007–009

THE DWARKS MEET THE TRASH MONSTER
A Bantam Skylark Book / September 1984

*Skylark Books is a registered trademark
of Bantam Books, Inc.
Registered in U.S. Patent and Trademark Office
and elsewhere.*

*All rights reserved.
Text, illustrations, and cover art copyright © 1984 by
Michael Berenstain.
This book may not be reproduced in whole or in part, by
mimeograph or any other means, without permission.
For information address: Bantam Books, Inc.*

ISBN 0-553-15288-2

Published simultaneously in the United States and Canada

*Bantam Books are published by Bantam Books, Inc. Its trade-
mark, consisting of the words "Bantam Books" and the por-
trayal of a rooster, is Registered in U.S. Patent and Trademark
Office and in other countries. Marca Registrada. Bantam
Books, Inc., 666 Fifth Avenue, New York, New York 10103.*

PRINTED IN THE UNITED STATES OF AMERICA

CW   0 9 8 7 6 5 4 3 2

It was autumn in the dump. The wind whistled through the trash, and a harvest moon rose over the Dwarks' old car home.

Inside, it was cozy and warm.

Momma Dwark worked on her knitting, and Poppa Dwark puffed on his corncob pipe. Big brother Yolo played Parcheesi with Granny while the Dwarklets wrestled on the floor.

Momma looked up at the clock and put down her knitting.

"It's getting late," she told the Dwarklets. "Time for bed!"

"Aw, Momma!" they complained. "It's not late—we're not sleepy yet!"

"It's way past your bedtime," she said firmly, turning down their bed.

"But we don't *wanna* go to bed!" they whined.

Granny looked up from her game.

"Don't you young 'uns know," she asked, "just what happens to Dwarklets who won't go to bed when they're told?"

"No," said the Dwarklets. "What?"

Granny leaned forward in her rocker.

"Why," she answered softly, "the *Trash Monster* comes an' gits 'em, that's what!"

"Trash Monster?" repeated the Dwarklets, a little frightened. "What's that?"

Granny rocked back and forth in her chair.

"The Trash Monster," she began, "is a huge, hairy creature that haunts the dump. It has glowing red eyes, sharp white teeth, and long yellow claws."

She raised her arms and bared her teeth.

"Ulp!" gulped the Dwarklets.

"By day," continued Granny, "it sleeps in its lair beneath the trash, but by night, it rises up to stalk the dump in search of food. It eats *anything*—bicycle tires, alley cats, Big Macs, vacuum cleaners, *and . . .*

"Yeow!" yelled the Dwarklets, jumping into bed and pulling the covers over their heads.

"Now, Granny," interrupted Momma, as she tucked the Dwarklets in, "there's really no such thing as a Trash Monster!"

"Oh, *no*?" asked Granny slyly. "Don't be too sure, my dear. . . .

Don't be *too* sure!"

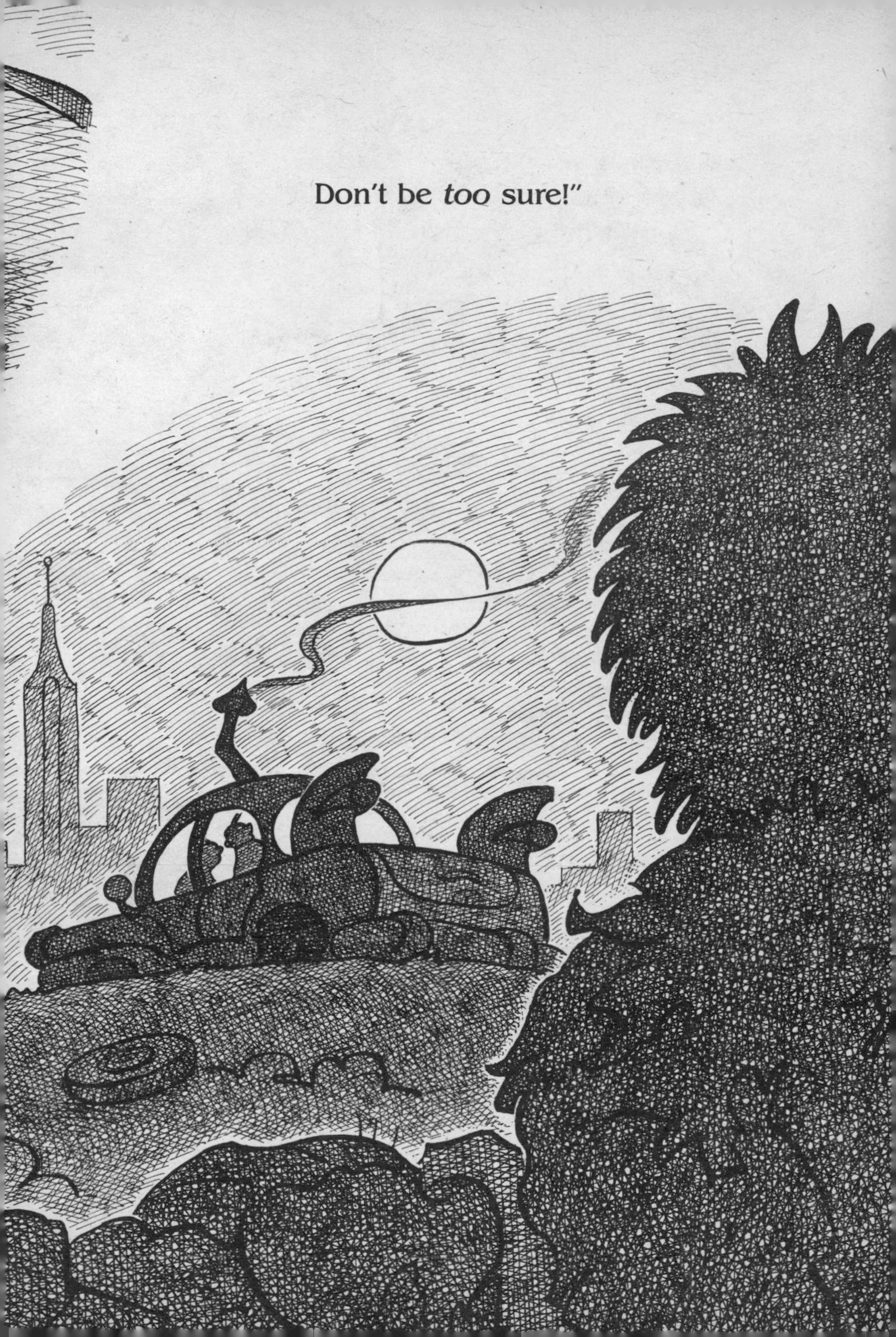

The next evening, the Dwarks were getting
ready for a big garbage raid.
Poppa checked their gear.
"Dwark trikes, check!
Salvage pails, check!
Possum masks, check!"
Granny watched from the doorway.

"You young 'uns
be careful,
now!" she warned.
"You never
can tell what
might be out there!"

"Don't you worry, Granny,"
said Poppa smugly. "Nothing
can go wrong while *I'm* in
charge!"

Momma rolled her eyes.

"O.K.!" said Poppa, lowering
his mask. "Let's roll!"

They pushed off and ped-
aled away.

Destination: HUMAN COUN-
TRY!

They ped-
aled across the
railroad tracks,

under the over-
pass, around
the drive-in,

behind the motel to . . .

THE DINER!
"Mmmmmmmm!" the Dwarklets
sighed. "Garbage!"

"Old spaghetti sauce!" whispered Yolo.

"Bacon grease!" Poppa drooled.

"Cold oatmeal!" Momma murmured.

They crept past the parked cars, past the brightly lit windows, past the kitchen exhaust fan—"Mmmmmmmm!" sighed the Dwarklets—around the back, to . . .

THE DUMPSTER!

"Wow!" said the Dwarklets. "Think of all the garbage in *there!*"

Poppa and Yolo held the ladder while the Dwarklets scrambled up.

They climbed to the top of the dumpster and peered in.

"Where's the food?" they asked.

But there wasn't any food!

No spaghetti sauce, no bacon grease, no cold oatmeal—just a big pile of old rags and blankets.

"What a bust!" the Dwarklets cried, sitting down on the heap. "We can't eat *this* stuff!"

Then, as they were sitting feeling sorry for themselves, they felt something move—something behind them!

They turned around, and peering over their shoulders they saw . . .

TWO GLOWING RED EYES!
"YEOW!" the Dwarklets yelled.
"It's the TRASH MONSTER!"

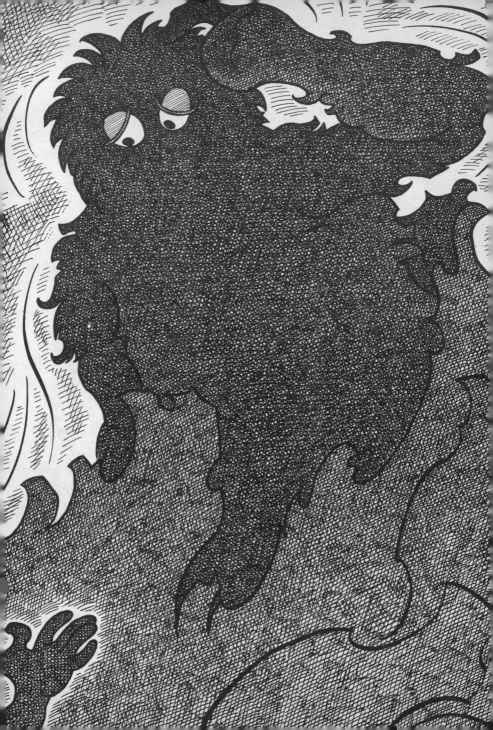

"Run!" the Dwarklets cried, as they dashed down the ladder.

The Dwarks jumped back on their trikes and pedaled away.

MOTEL

DINER

They pedaled behind the motel . . .

around the drive-in, un-
der the overpass, across
the railroad tracks . . .

and back to the dump.

"We saw it!" they gasped when
they were safe at home. "*The
Trash Monster!*"

"Trash Monster!" cried Granny. "Where?!"

"Over by the diner!" they panted, leaning on the door.

"The diner, eh?" mused Granny, rubbing her chin.

She marched over to her trunk and began to rummage through her things.

"What are you doing?" asked Momma.

"Gettin' ready!" she replied, tossing out ropes and nets and traps.

"What for?" asked Yolo, scratching his head.

"Why, the Trash Monster, of course!" she replied. "Didn't I tell you he roams the night in search of food? He'll be *here* next!"

"HERE?!" they all cried, diving under the table.

"Yup!" replied Granny, hauling her gear to the door. "We've got to get ready. Lend a hand!"

Under Granny's direction, the Dwarks built a complete early warning system around the dump. Anything that tried to get in would set off a terrific racket of tin cans, soda bottles, and rusty toasters.

The Dwarks patrolled the dump, armed to the teeth with plungers, eggbeaters, and butterfly nets.

All was quiet.

Then, just before dawn . . .

the alarm went off!

"It's over there, in Sector Eight!" yelled Granny.

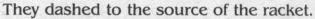

They dashed to the source of the racket.

"Now, where's that critter got himself to?"
wondered Granny, looking around.

"There he is!" cried the Dwarklets.

"Get him!" yelled Granny.

The Trash Monster pulled himself loose and ran away.

The Dwarks chased the Trash Monster.

The Trash Monster chased the Dwarks.

The Dwarks chased each other.

Finally, they lost track of the Trash Monster near the old packing crate.

"Careful, now!" warned Granny, as they backed around the crate. "He's around here somewhere!"

"YEEOOW!"

The Dwarks ducked into the crate.

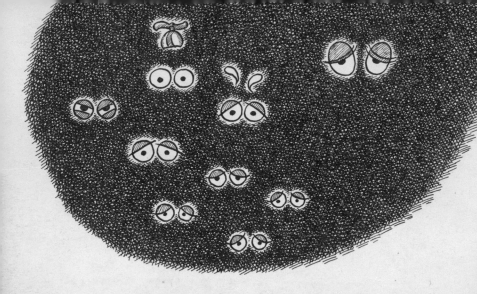

"Whew!" said Poppa. "That was close! At least we're safe in here!"

"Yeah," agreed Yolo, "all nine of us!"

"Nine?" asked Poppa.

"Sure!" said Yolo. "Me, you, Momma, Granny, the four Dwarklets, and . . ."

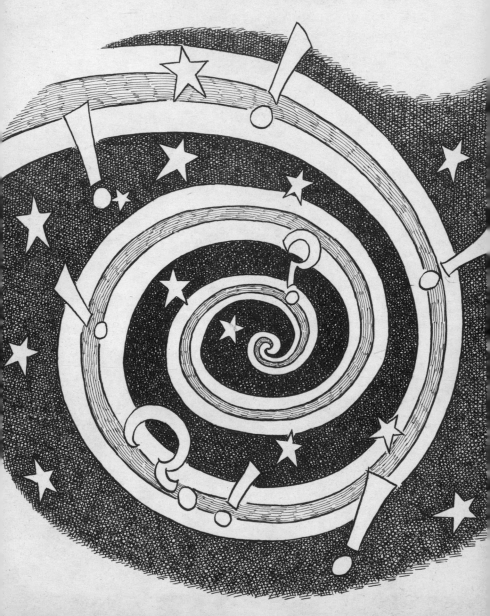

Momma lit a match.

A strange creature was cowering on the floor.

"What's *this*?" asked Momma, peering down at it. "It doesn't *look* like a monster!"

"D-d-don't hurt me!" it whimpered. "I'm innocent!"

"Why," exclaimed Momma, "it's a *human*!"

She took him by the arm and raised him to his feet.

"Don't be frightened," she said. "We won't hurt you. We thought you were the Trash Monster!"

"Trash Monster? *Me?*" exclaimed the human. "Why, I'm just old Bert, the tramp! I thought *you* was Dump Devils!"

"Dump Devils?" said Poppa. "No, we're Dwarks."

"Oh, that's a relief!" cried Bert, mopping his brow. "I thought you was Dump Devils, for sure!"

"Would you like some breakfast?" asked Momma.

"That's right neighborly of you," said the tramp. "Don't mind if I do."

So they took the tramp home and fixed him breakfast.

"Tasty!" exclaimed Bert, digging into the Dwarks' food. "Mighty tasty!"

"You know," he said, looking around, "this is a nice place you've got here—sort of reminds me of home!"

He cleaned his plate and got to his feet.

"Well," he said, patting his stomach, "I'm off! Got work to do. Come around and see me sometime. I'm right behind the diner in the big green dumpster—you can't miss it!"

"Good-bye!" The Dwarks waved.

"So long!" called Bert.

"You know," said Momma as they watched him
go, "Bert seems different from other humans."

"We *like* him!" exclaimed the Dwarklets. "He's
just like us!"

"Yes." Poppa nodded wisely. . . .

"Who would have thought that a human being could be so *advanced*?"

ABOUT THE AUTHOR

Born in 1951, Michael Berenstain grew up in the Philadelphia area, where he spent most of his childhood collecting insects.

Under the influence of his parents, Stan and Jan—the well-known artists and authors—his attentions soon shifted to painting and illustration, subjects which he studied at the Philadelphia College of Art and the Pennsylvania Academy of Fine Arts.

After working in the children's department of a New York publisher, he began working as a freelance author and illustrator.

His books include the *Castle, Ship, Lighthouse,* and *Armor* books, as well as the fanciful *Troll Book, Sorcerer's Scrapbook,* and *The Creature Catalog.*

He presently lives with his wife, Andrea, in Bucks County, Pennsylvania.